LENNY LEMMON and the Alien Invasion

illustrated by
JAMES LANCETT

nosy crow

Have you read?

LENNY LEMMON and the *Invincible Rat*

LENNY LEMMON and the **Trail of Crumbs**

FOR HESTER

B. D.

FOR OLLIE,
MY LITTLE ROCKET MAN.

J. L.

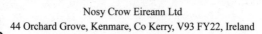

First published in the UK in 2024 by Nosy Crow Ltd
Wheat Wharf, 27a Shad Thames, London, SE1 2XZ, UK

Nosy Crow Eireann Ltd
44 Orchard Grove, Kenmare, Co Kerry, V93 FY22, Ireland

Nosy Crow and associated logos are trademarks
and/or registered trademarks of Nosy Crow Ltd.

Text copyright © Ben Davis, 2024
Cover and illustrations copyright © James Lancett, 2024

The right of Ben Davis and James Lancett to be identified as the author
and illustrator respectively of this work has been asserted by them
in accordance with the Copyright, Designs and Patents Act 1988.

ISBN: 978 1 80513 146 5

A CIP catalogue record for this book will be available from the British Library.

Printed and bound in Great Britain by Clays Ltd, Elcograf S.p.A.
following rigorous ethical sourcing standards.

Papers used by Nosy Crow are made from wood grown in sustainable forests.

MIX
Paper | Supporting
responsible forestry
FSC
www.fsc.org   FSC® C018072

1 3 5 7 9 10 8 6 4 2
www.nosycrow.com

BOOOORED. Bored, bored, bored.

People say school holidays are the most fun part of the year, but this one? BLAH. The longest two weeks EVER! It doesn't help that my two best friends, Sam and Jess, are both on holiday. Not together. Sam has gone to the seaside and Jess says she's rock climbing in the GOBI DESERT, even though our parents are friends and Mum says they're definitely in Tenerife.

I'm lying on the sofa trying to block out my brother Brandon's BUM-ACHINGLY BAD music thumping from upstairs, but I can't do it. I start poking at my wobbly tooth with my tongue. Maybe if it drops out, the tooth fairy can bring me something exciting.

CLUNK!

The noise comes from the basement. Dad's inventions lab is down there and we've had more explosions than a fireworks-testing factory just lately. Still, I'm so

BOOOOOORED

that I'm going down to see what's happening.

At the bottom of the basement stairs, the floor is covered in broken inventions. There are the legs from his **LOLLIPOP-MAN ROBOT** that fell apart outside my school and made a load of Year One kids cry.

There is the command console from his Chessmaster computer, which only knew how to play Hungry Hungry Hippos. And isn't that the bumper from the **HOVER CAR** that didn't hover?

As I pick my way through, I find Dad standing by his desk, writing something down. "Improve eye sockets," he mumbles as he writes.

"Everything OK, Dad?" I ask.

"Stupendous," he replies. "Just putting the finishing touches to my TRANSLATION HELMET."

Dad picks a helmet up from his desk. It's black and shiny with blinking red lights all over it.

"THIS IS GOING TO BE THE ONE, MY BOY," he says. "IT'S GOING TO CHANGE THE WORLD!"

Dad says that about all his inventions. But one day he might be right! Maybe.

"This bad boy instantly translates anything into the language of your choice," he says. "Watch this. I'm going to say, 'Hello, I would

like three eggs, please' in French and the translation helmet will say it in English."

Dad puts the helmet on his head and a weird robot voice crackles out.

"OWOH! ME WOO LIKEYLIKE THREEZY EGGYWEGGIES PLAZAZAZA."

Dad whips the helmet back off with a big grin. "Pretty cool, eh?"

I give him a thumbs up. "BRILLIANT!"

"And that's not all!"

"Really?" I say.

Dad nods, a proud smile still on his face. "Let's go upstairs."

THE GRAND REVEAL

In the back garden, something is covered in a sheet. I'm a bit nervous because last time Dad kept something under a sheet it was his AUTOMATIC HAIRCUTTING MACHINE, which gave him a wonky mohawk.

"Lenny, do you like biking?" he asks.

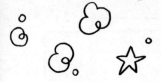

I nod. "Sometimes."

"And do you ever find yourself biking along and wishing you could go faster? And **HIGHER?**"

Now I'm interested. "Actually, yes!" I say. I don't tell him I often have a daydream about soaring above school and dropping water bombs on Mr Greenford, the head teacher.

"Introducing, the **FLYING BIKE!**"

Dad whips off the sheet to reveal a bike that looks a lot like mine, but with some added bits. Hang on a second. That IS mine!

"Dad, why have you messed with my bike?" I moan.

"Messed with?" says Dad. "I think you'll find the correct word is 'IMPROVED MASSIVELY'."

He grins at me and I stare back at him. "I think that might be TWO words."

Dad laughs. "Take a look!" He points at the handlebars. On one side there's a dial that has

written beside it. On the other side,

there's a big red button that says

"Come on, watch me take her for a test drive," he says.

Two minutes later, Dad is sitting on my bike in the middle of our road, wearing a motorcycle helmet, and pads on his knees and elbows. Now, this could be **EXCITING!** Imagine if it works! Every shop in the world is going to want these: the Lemmon Flying Bike! We'll be so rich, I won't even have to go to school any more. Better yet, I could

BUY the school. Imagine if I were the head teacher. First up, I'm banning maths.

"LENNY!"

Dad yells, snapping me out of my daydream. "I said are you ready to start filming? This could be a historic moment!"

I press record on Mum's phone and give him the thumbs up. Dad nods and gives me a thumbs up back. He turns the dial and starts pootling down the street. When he gets to the end, he spins round and comes back. I hear him scream, **"TURBO THREE!"**

The bike heads back towards me faster. I see him crank the dial. "FOUR!"

My heart pounds so loud it almost drowns out the roar of the bike.

"TURBO FIVE!" Dad yells.

"FLY, FLY, FLY!"

Dad smashes the big red button and the bike jumps up. I whoop with delight. **IT'S WORKING!** We're going to change the world!

Then the bike clunks back down and smacks into the kerb. Dad goes flying over the handlebars and lands in Mrs Patel's flowerbed. I run over to him, scared that he's hurt himself, but he climbs to his feet with daffodils sticking out of his motorcycle helmet.

"It's fine," he says. "Just needs a little tweaking, that's all."

I look down at my bike, lying in a twisted heap in the road.

"Or maybe a **BIG** tweaking."

After Dad's failed experiment I was still **BORED,** so he gave me a whisk to take back to Grandma's shop. He had used it to make a Whiskatron robot the other day, but it refused to whisk. Then it escaped the kitchen and went **FACE-FIRST** into a pond.

I had to go the long way round because the bridge over Duggler's Ditch, which is a huge dry stream, has been demolished before they start work on a new one.

Linda Lemmon's Ice Cream Parlour has been in town since forever. I bet

DINOSAURS

used to go there for knickerbocker glories. It's my favourite place, and not just because I get free ice creams.

I walk in and it's the same as always: Grandma's favourite olden-days music

playing, all the chairs and tables squeaky clean, and the counter cabinet piled high with **EVERY KIND OF ICE CREAM** you can think of. My favourite thing to do is to grab a cone and stack it with **FOUR** different scoops: chocolate, chocolate chip, white chocolate and chocolate crunch. All the varieties. I call it the Patented Trademark Lenny Lemmon Quadruple Super Scooper.

"**HI, GRANDMA!**" I yell, making her jump as she leans on the counter reading a book. "I brought your whisk back!"

Grandma takes a look at the whisk, all caked in mud, and drops it into the bin.

"Thank you, Lenny," she sighs.

It isn't like Grandma to be sad. She's the happiest person I know, normally. "What's the matter, Grandma? Is it the dirty whisk?"

Grandma shakes her head and waves her hand around the shop. "It's this place, my love. Look at it."

I take a look around and shrug. "What's wrong with it?"

"Don't you think there's something **MISSING?**" she says.

"Now you mention it," I say, "I've always thought you should do burgers and chips."

"Not burgers and chips, Lenny. People!"

I gasp. "You can't eat people!"

Grandma sighs again. "I mean **NO ONE** is here. You know, I haven't even sold one ice cream today? Not a single solitary scoop."

"Why?" I ask. "Your ice cream is **DELICIOUS.**"

Grandma snatches up a cloth and starts cleaning the counter, even though I can already see my face in it.

"It's that EnormoMall they opened outside town last year," she says. "They have ice cream from all around the world there." She stops scrubbing and squeezes my hand. "If this carries on, I'm afraid I'm going to have to close the shop."

NO! That is unthinkable. Grandma has worked there her entire life. It holds so many family memories. I'M GOING TO HAVE TO DO SOMETHING.

THE BOOK SHOP

I'm SO sad, I even forget to take a Patented Trademark Lenny Lemmon Quadruple Super Scooper for the journey home.

Sam's family own a bookshop just around the corner from Grandma's place, and when I walk past I'm surprised to see his dad putting books on shelves. **HUH.** I go inside.

"**HI, SAM'S DAD!**" I say.

He smiles when he sees me. "Ah, Lenny! Come to take him out playing, have you?"

I frown. "But he's on holiday!"

"I can assure you he isn't. I—"

"SSSH!"

Sam's dad is interrupted by a weird noise coming from the children's section round the corner.

"Sam's dad," I say nervously. "Is there a snake in the kids' books?"

Sam's dad chuckles. "Why don't you go and have a look?"

"NO!" a little voice bleats from the same place.

I slowly walk round the corner and find nothing but a load of books and a cardboard cut-out of a dragon. To begin with, I think the dragon is speaking and I'm worried it's going to shoot fire at me, but then I see a shoe sticking out from behind it. Sure enough, there he is.

"SAM!"

Sam comes out from his hiding place and slumps on to a purple beanbag. "Fine. You caught me."

"But I don't understand. You told me you were going on **HOLIDAY**."

Sam's bottom lip droops. "We were supposed to be, but then we didn't."

"So I've been bored on my own all week when we could have been **PLAYING?!**" I say. "Don't you like me any more, Sam?"

Sam fiddles with the collar of his shirt, like he always does when he's worried. "It's not that." He lowers his voice to a whisper. "It's because we couldn't afford to go and I was too **EMBARRASSED** to tell you."

I sit on a little plastic stool next to him. It makes a farting sound and I can't help but giggle a bit. "You don't need to be **EMBARRASSED** in front of me, Sam. We're best friends, remember?

SPIT SWEAR FOREVER!"

Sam nods and his eyes go all wet. "Sorry, Lenny."

"You don't need to be **SORRY** either." I pull a crocodile puppet off a toy rack and put it on my hand, making it talk in a growly voice. "Now, let's go out and play. **AND MAKE IT SNAPPY!**"

Sam smiles a little bit at my brilliant joke. "I'm just scared, Lenny."

"Of the crocodile?" I say. "I can put it away if you want."

"No, not the crocodile." Sam leans in close and whispers even softer. "I heard Mum and Dad talking about the shop. They said that no one comes into town any more and they're not selling any books. They're worried they'll have to close."

"It's the EnormoMall!" I say, shaking my crocodiley fist.

Sam nods. "Dad says all the shops will close soon and the whole place will be a **GHOST TOWN.**"

My eyes go fuzzy as I imagine it: ghost cafés, ghost hairdressers. I wonder what it would be like to have a ghost cut your hair? **HAIR-RAISING,** I bet! Haha!

"LENNY!" Sam clicks in my face, interrupting my daydream. "He doesn't mean an actual town full of ghosts. He means no one will be here."

I think about it for a second. That sounds horrible. I can't imagine the town without Grandma's ice cream shop and Sam's dad's bookshop and the toy shop and the market where scary people shout weird stuff about vegetables.

"Sam," I say, putting my arm round his shoulder. "WE ARE NOT GOING TO LET THAT HAPPEN."

Sam shakes his head. "Come on, Lenny,

we're just kids. What are we going to do?"

I jump to my feet and throw my hands in the air. "We are going to **SAVE THE TOWN!**"

Sam sighs. "I'd take you more seriously if one of your hands wasn't a crocodile."

I throw the puppet off and sit back down next to Sam. "Listen, we saved the school, didn't we?"

"Well, not real—"

"**WE DID,**" I say. "**AND** we won the Olden Days competition for class 5B."

"Again, it was a little more complicated than that."

"**BABABABA!**" I hold up my hand, not

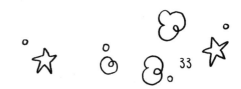

wanting to hear about complicated stuff. "Anything is possible, Samuel. **ANYTHING**."

I lean forwards and shout into the main part of the shop.

"Sam's dad! Sam is having a **SLEEPOVER** at my house tonight!"

"Um, OK?" he replies.

"Excellent," I say, pumping my fist. "Now, come on, Sam. Grab your toothbrush and your **THINKING CAP**, because we've got some planning to do."

Sam yawns and rubs his eyes while I stare at
a sheet of paper that says

"WAYS TO
SAVE THE TOWN"

and nothing else. Well, except a doodle of me as a big muscleman.

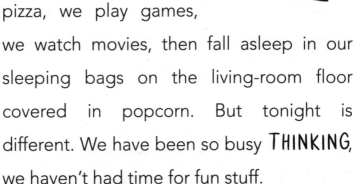

Normally, sleepovers with me and Sam are **MASSIVE FUN.** We eat pizza, we play games, we watch movies, then fall asleep in our sleeping bags on the living-room floor covered in popcorn. But tonight is different. We have been so busy THINKING, we haven't had time for fun stuff.

"Come on, Sam," I say. "You're the one

with the good school-report cards. Surely you can think of something?"

Sam yawns again. "We could give people money to go into town?"

I rub my chin. "And where would we get this money?"

"I have some coins in my piggy bank?" he says.

"How many?" I say. "A million?"

Sam narrows his eyes and counts on his fingers. "Nine, I think."

This is no good. We need to think of something that will drag people away from the EnormoMall and back to the fun books at Sam's place and the delicious ice cream at Grandma's.

Something **BIG**. Something **BOLD**.

Maybe TV will give us some inspiration. I turn it on and it automatically goes to the SCI-FI CHANNEL. Dad must have been the last one in here. He's forever watching boring shows about space, where people with ridgey heads are always firing lasers at a bald man's ship. That's not on now though. It's showing a stretch of desert with some metal stuff strewn across it.

"What's this?" says Sam sleepily.

I press the button. *"Alien Encounters."*

The screen changes to a small American town in the middle of nowhere. A man with crazy hair and a **WILD** look in his eyes comes on.

"No one had ever heard of Roswell before the flying saucer crashed here," he says. "Then all of a sudden the whole world shows up."

We watch for a little longer and it's true. Ages and ages ago, people reckoned an **ALIEN SPACESHIP** crashed in this tiny town called Roswell and it's still famous to this day.

All the shops sell alien stuff and people come from all over to see it.

Sam chuckles. "That's what we need. Some **ALIENS** to crash their ship here."

I laugh too, and put on an alien voice. "Yes, please, Mr or Miss Alien. **COME CRASH HERE!** It's way nicer than Neptune!"

"Or Pluto," Sam laughs.

"OR **URANUS!**"

We laugh and laugh until tears are rolling down our cheeks, but then I suddenly stop. An idea has hit me like a bad pie flying across the school canteen.

Sam's laugh comes to a stuttering stop

and he looks at me. "Lenny?" he says, sounding worried.

"But what if..."

"Lenny, you're pulling that face..."

"What if we didn't **NEED** the aliens to actually come here?"

"You're pulling that face you always pull when you're hatching one of your schemes."

"What if people just **THOUGHT** aliens had come?"

"Lenny, NO. **NO!**"

THE CRASH

"LENNY, I'M SCARED," Sam whispers as we step out of my house into the dark, cold night.

I give him one of my trademark reassuring shoulder slaps, but softly, so it doesn't wake anyone. "RELAX," I say. "There's no way this could possibly go wrong."

"You say that so often it's lost all meaning," Sam moans.

As soon as the idea hatched in my brain, like a **TINY DUCKLING OF PURE GENIUS**, the rest of it followed quickly. You see, for most people, faking a UFO crash would be tricky, but me? With Dad's basement full of failed invention parts just lying around? So many of them that he won't even notice if a few go missing? It would be crazy not to!

The woods opposite Grandma's shop are only a few minutes' walk away. The tricky part will be avoiding being seen with our two

wheelbarrows full of clanking metal parts. Best to take it slowly.

Even over the sound of the barrows I can still hear Sam's teeth **CHATTERING**.

"It's going to be fine," I say, as we turn the corner at the end of my road and head towards town. "Just think about how well your dad's

shop's going to do once this all goes off. You'll be able to have the **FANCIEST HOLIDAYS EVER!** I'm talking tropical safari hotels, with gorilla waiters ... and sloth maids ... and pool lifeguards that are ... sharks? No, that wouldn't work—"

Oh no. I was too busy thinking about the tropical safari hotel and I've clunked my wheelbarrow into a kerb and tipped it over and now some of the stuff has **SPILLED** on to someone's garden.

"**LENNY!**" Sam gasps.

I put my wheelbarrow right and start loading the stuff back in.

"**WHO GOES THERE?**"

The front door of the house opens and a man leans out.

"**GO, GO, GO!**" I whisper-shout at Sam.

We run with our wheelbarrows as fast as we can away from him.

"HE'S CHASING US, LENNY!" Sam pants at me.

I take a quick look over my shoulder and, sure enough, here he comes FLAPPING after us in his slippers. This was not part of the plan at all. If he sees what we have in our wheelbarrows it might ruin the whole thing. I have to think of a way out of this.

"Sam," I whisper, then jerk my head towards an alleyway next to me. I know you can get to the woods that way. It will mean going to a deeper, DARKER part than

I was planning, but at least we'll be there.

We clatter down the lane and park our wheelbarrows behind a huge tree. The man's footsteps don't get any closer.

"OK," I say. "I think we're safe."

EEEEEeeeAAAAAOOWWWW.

A low noise, like a cross between a growl and a purr, comes from right behind us. Sam **SCREAMS** and the noise happens again, this time louder.

"Lenny, what was that?" Sam whispers.

I think for a second it might be a **BIGFOOT**.

Bigfeet are these enormous **HAIRY APEMEN** and, legend has it, they live in the woods. That rumour probably started when someone saw my brother Brandon there.

BIGFOOT
~~BRANDON~~

EEEEEEEEAAAAAOOWWWWW.

We slowly turn around and see, lit by the moonlight, a badger slinking towards us.

"AWWW, LOOK AT THAT!" I say, super relieved it isn't some mythical beast. "What a little cutie!" I reach out to stroke it but it snarls and

SNAPS at me, baring its teeth.

"What is it with **ME AND RODENTS?**" I gasp, speedily whipping my hand back.

"Badgers aren't rodents, they're mustelidae," Sam squeaks, terrified. "We must be near its sett. I've heard they can get –" he gulps – "**NASTY** when you get near their setts."

The badger advances on us, still GROWLING with bared teeth. "OK, I think I know what to do," I say. "I read it once. You're supposed to stay perfectly still. That way, they can't see you."

"Are you sure that's badgers, Lenny?" Sam whimpers. "Are you sure you're not thinking of TYRANNOSAURUS REXES?"

I think about it for a second. "Maybe you're right."

The badger snarls and SNAPS as it

creeps closer. We both step back but our wheelbarrows clash. Aha! **THAT'S IT!** I reach into mine and pull out the arm from Dad's Beauty Spa Robot, which blew up while it was rubbing his feet.

"Stay back!" I say. "Or I'll, um, massage you?"

The badger leaps up, grabs the arm and rips it out of my hands.

"**I HATE NATURE!**" Sam cries.

It looks like the badger is about to strike again when...

WHHEEEEEEEEEEEEEEEEEEE!

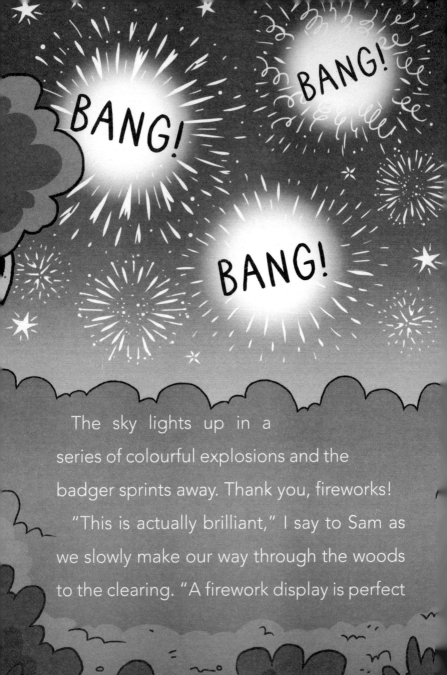

The sky lights up in a
series of colourful explosions and the
badger sprints away. Thank you, fireworks!
"This is actually brilliant," I say to Sam as
we slowly make our way through the woods
to the clearing. "A firework display is perfect

cover for a spaceship crash. All the noise and lights. OK, now the real work starts."

We use spades to scrape dirt away and create the illusion of a crash, then scatter a load of metal and electric stuff around. It's so dark, it's hard to tell if it looks good. We stand there for a second and admire our handiwork.

"Do you really think this will work?" says Sam, chewing his thumbnail.

I put my arm around him and give him a squeeze. "Sam. There's no way it can fail."

EEEEEEEEAAAAAOOWWWWW!

Oh no.

ALIEN FEVER!

"What did I tell you?" I say to Sam as we stand at the back of the **ENORMOUS CROWD** in the woods. "Worked like a charm!"

It's going even better than I thought, no doubt helped by another **GENIUS** idea

I came up with after we sneaked back into my room last night.

I grabbed Mum's phone from downstairs and downloaded **FLIPFLOP**. You know, that video app with all the dancing and stuff? I made a really quick video on there showing the crash. It was super easy to do, just some **LASER THINGIES** and an explosion **SOUND EFFECT**, but it was enough to make people believe. Now it feels like everyone in town is here.

"Maybe it's just some **RUBBISH?**" a man says.

"Look at it though," says a woman standing next to him. "It's all so

It can only have come from a flying saucer."

Or my dad's lab.

We leave the woods and walk across the road to the town centre. The car park is **PACKED** and there are more people walking the streets than I've seen in ages. Crowds all the way up to Duggler's Ditch.

We stop by Grandma's ice cream shop, but we can't get in because the **QUEUE** is nearly out of the door. I can see Grandma behind the counter and she has a **HUGE SMILE** on her face. I almost want to tell her that me and Sam did all this, but it has to be our secret.

We head down to Sam's dad's bookshop and that's full too.

"**WOW,**" Sam whispers, and his eyes go all big and wet.

"What did I tell you, my friend?" I say. "You can always rely on your old mate Lenny to sort things out."

THE LAST FEW DAYS HAVE BEEN CRAZY. People from all over have been flocking to town to see the alien crash site, and while they're here they're treating themselves to ice creams, and Sam's dad has had to keep ordering in **ALIEN** books

because they're flying off the shelves.

Me and Sam are in town now, watching all the people arrive. There are **TV CREWS** here and everything, and I keep walking behind the people they're talking to and **PULLING FUNNY FACES** until eventually a pink-faced woman in headphones yells at me to stop.

A long black car pulls up and a man in a suit steps out. He doesn't seem like he's here to enjoy the town and talk about aliens. His face is **MEAN**, with a big down-turned mouth. He looks like what would happen if a pug and a toad had an **EVIL MANBABY**.

"All right, let's make this quick, shall we?"

he says to Headphones Woman. "Some of us have important businesses to run."

He looks me and Sam up and down. Sam has a big gloop of caramel ice cream on his chin and I should probably tell him.

"You two LITTLE OIKS better not do anything to my car," he says.

The camera starts up and someone with a microphone talks to EVIL TOADPUG man. "Sir Percival Hickenbottom, you are the chairman of the EnormoMall just outside town. What do you make of all this?"

The man looks around at the street, and I see his nasty eyes land on Grandma's shop.

"It's hogwash. Piffle. Poppycock. There is **NO SUCH THING** as aliens."

"Well, what do you say about the crash site?" says Microphone Man. "A lot of people are convinced."

Hickenbottom **LAUGHS,** but it's not a nice laugh. It sounds like a crow with the flu. "If you told these people horses pooped gold, they'd be at your nearest farm with **BUCKETS IN THEIR HANDS** before you could blink."

"So you're saying the people here are stupid?" says Microphone Man.

"Nooo, no, no, not stupid!" says Sir Percy. "Just GULLIBLE."

That's it. I've heard enough. I hold my arms out wide, then puff out my cheeks, cross my eyes and SIDEWAYS-WALK behind Sir Percy like a crab. I can't tell because my eyes are all blurry, but I'm pretty sure Headphones Woman is FRANTICALLY WAVING at me to go away. But I'm not going to. This man was about to turn our town

into a dead zone with his EnormoMall and now he's being mean to us. I sneak a look at Sam and he's turned the colour of milk.

"For one thing, if an alien spaceship has crashed here, **WHERE ARE THE ALIENS**, eh? It couldn't have got here by itself, could it?" he goes on.

"It might!" I say. "Maybe their technology is really good."

Hickenbottom turns around and eyeballs me. "Who asked **YOU** anyway, you little rotter?"

I can't think of anything to say, so I just stick out my tongue.

"What would convince you?" says Microphone Man. "**REAL PROOF** of aliens here on Earth?"

Sir Percy lets another dry chuckle go: "If anyone finds genuine evidence of aliens here, **I WILL EAT MY HAT.**"

"But you're not wearing a hat!" I chip in.

"I'm a **VERY WEALTHY MAN**," he booms back at me. "I could buy the most expensive hat in the shop and eat it like it's a lasagne. That's how sure I am that

THERE IS NO SUCH THING AS ALIENS!"

I crabwalk back to Sam and **NUDGE** him in the ribs.

"You know what we have to do now, don't you?" I say.

Sam sighs.

"PLEASE NO,"

he says. "I'm begging you."

PROOF

"If anyone sees us, this is for a **SCHOOL PROJECT**," I say, pushing the green papier mâché alien head down on top of Sam's.

A few months ago we made these heads in class. They were supposed to be **SELF-PORTRAITS** but no one actually

looked like them. Not even **MISS PERFECT** Amelia Kelly. Anyway, last night Sam and I found ours and slathered them in green paint.

"**CAN WE MAKE THIS QUICK?**" he says, his voice sounding all weird and boomy.

"You can't rush GENIUS, Samuel," I say.

We're standing in the deepest part of the woods, surrounded by thick trees. I have Mum's phone again, ready to make a FlipFlop video that will prove the existence of aliens in our town and leave SIR STINKYBOTTOM with no choice but to chow down on his best top hat.

I'm thinking the video will have to be filmed from PRETTY FAR AWAY. Otherwise other kids from our class might notice that we made the head as an art project a few weeks ago.

I step back and perch on a tree stump,

holding up the phone. "OK, Sam," I say. "Start acting **ALIEN-Y.**"

As well as the head, he's wearing tight green joggers, a green jumper and green gloves.

SUPER COOL.

Sam looks at me. Well, he doesn't **LOOK** at me because the head has no eyeholes, but he's kind of facing in the right direction. **"WHAT DO YOU MEAN?** What do aliens act like?"

I shrug. "Walk around with your arms out?"

"That's what **MUMMIES** and **ZOMBIES** do," says Sam.

"OK, well, then just walk normally," I say.

Sam starts walking with his arms out in front of him.

"Hold on, I thought only zombies and mummies did that," I say.

"YES, BUT I CAN'T SEE WHERE I'M GOING, LENNY!"

I film Sam walking, being careful to only get him from the side or back. I'm about to watch it back, when...

CRUNCH, CRUNCH, CRUNCH.

Oh no, someone's coming!

"Hide!" I whisper to Sam. He runs and crouches behind some bushes.

A figure gets closer, and I can see it has a dog on a lead, and there's something familiar about the dog in the way it is panting and straining. **SURELY NOT!**

"Lenny?" says my head teacher, Mr Greenford. "What are you doing in the middle of the woods?"

I CAN'T BELIEVE IT! Of all the people to run into here, why him?

"I suppose I could ask you the same question," I fire back.

Mr Greenford's bushy eyebrows SHOOT SKYWARDS and his face goes purple like he's about to order me to go to his office, but then he seems to remember that we're not in school and calms down a bit.

"I'm taking CRUMBS for his morning walk, if you must know," he says, nodding at our school dog, Crumbs, who is pulling so hard to get to me, his EYEBALLS are nearly popping out.

"Now, how about you? Quite interesting that you're here on your own," he says.

I **SHRUG** and try not to look at the outline of Sam huddled just behind Mr Greenford. At least the green blends in.

"You know me, Mr Greenford. I like to be part of nature!"

Mr Greenford **FROWNS** at me doubtfully as I notice Crumbs's nose twitching. Oh no.

"**HEY, CRUMBS!**" I yell. "Why don't you come and say hello?"

But Crumbs isn't listening to me. He's trying to get **BEHIND** Mr Greenford and is wrapping the lead around his legs.

Crumbs sniffs and **GROWLS**. He must have Sam's scent. I have to do something.

"Hey, Mr Greenford," I blurt. "Want to see something really **COOL** and nature-y?"

Mr Greenford tuts as he unwinds himself from the lead. "What do you mean?"

"Oh, I can't describe it," I say. "You have to see it to believe it. It's ... **EDUCATIONAL?**"

Crumbs's nose edges closer to Sam. I bet he can feel his breath and everything.

"<u>REALLY</u> EDUCATIONAL!"

Mr Greenford shakes his head. "OK, fine. Lead on."

We walk through the woods away from Sam. Crumbs keeps turning round and barking.

"Come along, Crumbs, **WHAT'S THE MATTER WITH YOU?**" Mr Greenford moans.

"Maybe there's a **BADGER SETT** nearby," I say. "We should be careful because they can get nasty if you invade their territory."

Mr Greenford looks shocked that I've come out with something educational. Speaking of which, this might do.

"Hey, look," I say, pointing at a tree with a big knobbly bit halfway up the trunk. "IT LOOKS LIKE A NOSE!"

Mr Greenford stares at me, still keeping a tight grip on Crumbs's lead.

"**THIS** is the educational thing you just *had* to show me?"

I nod. "Pretty cool, isn't it? Maybe we

could do a project about it at school."

"About a tree with a nose?" he says.

I nod again. "Yes, Mr Greenford."

Mr Greenford stares at me again. "I think you're

UP TO SOMETHING, LENNY."

I gasp like I'm **SHOCKED**. "Me, Mr Greenford? Since when am I ever up to things?"

Mr Greenford chuckles. "EVERY DAY, LENNY. Every day of my professional life." He stops and SQUINTS at me, rubbing his moustache. "This whole alien thing," he says. "That's not anything to do with you, is it?"

I gulp. "Of course not, Mr Greenford. Whatever gave you that idea?"

Mr Greenford takes a look around, his hand on his hip, but thankfully doesn't see Sam dressed as an alien, now curled up into a ball on the ground.

"Just call it a HUNCH," he says, walking on with Crumbs.

When Mr Greenford and Crumbs are out

of sight, I rush back to Sam, who whips off his papier mâché head.

"IS HE GONE?"

I nod. "We're safe now, Sam."

Something rustles in the leaves behind us, and I can tell it's not human. I've got a feeling I've heard it before though.

EEEEEeeeAAAAAOOWWWWW.

Not again.

THE RETURN

Exactly as I said it would, the alien FlipFlops
of Sam walking through the woods have sent

ALIEN FEVER

through the roof!

The town is **RAMMED** with tourists all the time. Like, right now we're in Grandma's ice cream parlour for a special **"ALIEN DAY"**. Grandma has changed the ice cream flavours so they're in keeping with the theme. There's **MARTIAN MINT, INTERSTELLAR SWIRL** and **COSMIC CRUNCH**, all of them drenched in sticky green syrup.

Business is **SO GOOD** that Grandma's allowed Dad to have a table in the corner showing off some of his inventions.

He has been working on the flying bike, but it's still no closer to taking off.

"I think it's the timing, Lenny," he says. "I feel like I need to hit Fly at the exact right moment when I get to TURBO FIVE, but I keep missing it."

Sam and I are enjoying our Patented Trademark Lenny Lemmon Quadruple Super Scoopers next to Dad's table, watching the curious onlookers.

"This?" says Dad to a lady with a baby strapped to her chest in a sling. "This is an ALIEN DETECTOR." He picks up what looks like a water pistol with a light attached to the end. I aim it at you, and if you're human, the light goes BLUE, but if you're an alien, it goes RED." He lifts it and points it at the woman, who flinches a little. The light goes bright blue. Dad nods. "You're safe."

I take a satisfied lick of the Scooper and smile at Sam. "We did it, my friend. Yet again, the Caped Crusaders save the day!"

Sam frowns. "But we don't wear capes."

"Good point. How about ... the POWER PALS?"

"Not keen," says Sam.

"THE TERRIFIC TWOSOME?" I offer, but before Sam can respond I feel a PUNCH on my shoulder. I turn round and there is our friend **JESS**, arms folded.

"Twosome, is it?" she huffs.

"Oh hi, Jess! I didn't know you were back," I say, while Sam nervously waves.

"Well, I am," she says. "But it seems like you two were having a **PERFECTLY FUN TIME** without me." She looks around at the packed ice cream shop and raises her eyebrows at us.

"Yeah," I say. "Can you believe it?"

Jess shakes her head. "You two must think I'm stupid. As soon as I heard about this **ALIEN THING** when I was in Tener—" She stops and corrects herself. "The Gobi Desert, I knew you two must have something to do with it."

Sam gasps and I reach behind me and gently tap his arm. "Jess," I say, super slowly. "I have **NO IDEA** what you're talking about."

Of course I was planning on letting Jess in on the secret, but I can't admit to anything here. If someone hears, it's **GAME OVER**.

Jess laughs without smiling. "Oh, so that's how it's going to be, is it?"

89

"JESS," I say, waggling my eyebrows in a way I hope is telling her to calm down and that we'll talk about it later. "I DON'T KNOW WHAT YOU'RE TALKING ABOUT."

Jess turns her back on us and starts looking through Dad's inventions. She picks up a little microphone and asks Dad what it is.

"That's a voice changer," he says proudly. "Try it out!"

Jess holds it in front of her mouth and turns back to us.

"I THOUGHT WE WERE FRIENDS," says this weird robot voice.

"We are," I say, but my voice is drowned

out by a much louder one by the doors.

"CAN I HAVE YOUR ATTENTION, PLEASE?"

We all turn to see what's going on. Sir Percival Hickenbottom stands there with a face like a **WET CAMPING HOLIDAY** in a field full of angry cows with bad farts.

"When are you eating your hat, Perce?" someone in the crowd yells.

"**NEVER!**" he booms back. "Because those supposed 'alien sightings' are nothing more than a hoax! **AND I CAN PROVE IT!**

Tomorrow at eight p.m. I am holding a **PUBLIC MEETING** outside this shop where I will shut down all this talk of aliens once and for all. Then maybe you people will stop wasting your time in grubby little holes like this and come back to the EnormoMall!"

"THAT'S IT!"

Grandma slides across the counter and charges through the crowd holding her ice cream scoop up high and Sir Percival has to scarper before she **WALLOPS** him with it.

I waggle my eyebrows at Sam as if to say, "You know what we need to do."

He waggles his eyebrows back at me as if to say, "No, actually, **I DON'T.**"

INVASION!

"Lenny, I'm **SWEATING**," Sam complains as we approach the EnormoMall.

We're both wearing **GREEN ALIEN CLOTHES** with long, thick coats on over the top. It is only two hours until Sir Percival's big meeting outside Grandma's shop and

our mission is simple: stage an **ALIEN INVASION** of the EnormoMall and get it on FlipFlop before it starts.

Inside, the EnormoMall's enormous fans cool us down right away. Everything is white and shiny, and **RELAXING MUSIC** plays over the speakers.

"This is what I imagine Heaven to look like," I say to Sam. "Except there's an Apple Store and a lady doing eyebrows."

We stop by a **HUGE FOUNTAIN** with a golden statue of a naked man playing a trumpet.

"Phone?" I say.

I take out my mum's phone and Sam gets out the one he borrowed from the bookshop.

"HEAD?"

I hold up my bag, which contains a green papier mâché alien head, and Sam does the same.

"Any questions?"

"Yes," says Sam. "Do we have to?"

"Sam, how can we not?" I say. "Sir Percival is trying to bring down the ENTIRE THING. We need to show him it's for real."

Sam sighs. "But, Lenny?"

"Yes, Sam?"

"It's NOT for real."

"SSSSH!" I say, frantically looking around in case any of the shoppers going by heard him.

"That's not the point," I say. "If we want the town to STAY SAVED, we have to make people think it is."

"I know that," says Sam. "But surely if the aliens are seen at the EnormoMall, people will come here and town will be empty again?"

"No way," I say. "The CRASH SITE is in town. Besides, we can do loads more FlipFlops outside Grandma's and your dad's shops. Then if people visit town AND the

EnormoMall, Sir Perce will get off our backs."

I've given it lots of thought. It really is the **PERFECT** solution.

Sam gulps and shifts on his feet. "I still feel bad about Jess."

"**I DO TOO**," I say. "As soon as we've got this out of the way, we'll let her in on the secret."

I'm sure Jess will be fine with it once we come clean. She'll probably come up with all kinds of cool ideas to keep it going too. But for now, we have our mission: **DEFEAT SIR PERCIVAL HICKENBOTTOM.**

CLOSE ENCOUNTERS

We agreed that Sam should take the left-hand side of the EnormoMall while I take the right, and meet up by the fountain in **EXACTLY ONE HOUR**. It makes sense to split up, because that way we get to make more videos and cover more ground.

See, the thing about the EnormoMall is it's enormous.

I decide to start with an **EASY** one. Down a little side corridor that leads to a deserted candle shop there's a big poster on the wall that says:

ENORMOMALL

in giant letters. That's going to really boil Hickenbottom's parsnips. I set the phone up on top of a bin, ditch my giant coat, put on my head and do my best alien walk in front of it.

I watch it back afterwards. Pretty good! Once I add some **ALIEN EFFECTS** it will look cool.

"Can I help you?"

I freeze and look up. There's a man standing there, dressed all in black. He's wearing **SUNGLASSES** even though we're indoors, and his arms are like veiny tree trunks. I look down and see the top of the paper mâché head is poking out of the top of my bag, so I give it a nudge and it falls on its side.

"**NO, THANK YOU**," I say. "Just doing some shopping."

He points at my coat with two fingers.

"Just doing some **SHOPPING** in your **COAT,** are you?"

How weird. Why is he bothered about my coat? "Yes?" I say.

"Pretty **WARM** day today," he says. "What's the matter? **COLD-BLOODED?**"

Wait. Is he accusing me of being a lizard? "No," I say. "It's just my favourite coat."

The man walks closer and leans down to me.

He smells like aftershave and coffee and sweaty armpits. "Listen up, you little punk," he says. "I've been a store detective for twenty years and I know a THIEF when I see one."

I gasp and clamp a hand over my chest. "HOW RUDE! I have never stolen a thing in my life."

His mouth twists into a smirk. "That's what they all say. 'Oh, not ME, mister! I'm just an innocent shopper.' Then I check their pockets and  BOOM.

Chocolate bars out the wazoo."

I turn out my pockets, sending bits of lint, elastic bands and a note I was supposed to pass to Sam in class last year that says "AMELIA KELLY IS A DRACULA" fluttering to the floor.

"No chocolate here," I say. "Now, if you'll excuse me."

"Uh-huh," he says, standing up to his full height and crossing his WWE arms. "And how about the BAG?"

Oh no. I grab it and SCRUNCH it shut. "That's private."

"I'll bet it is. OPEN IT UP now," he growls.

I think about it. If I do as he says, he will

know the big secret. And I don't think he's the secret-keeping type.

"Um, no?" I say.

The man looks like he's just received an **ELECTRIC SHOCK** directly to his bum cheeks. "What did you just say?"

"It's private," I say, drawing the bag close to my body. "No one is allowed to see."

The man rubs his hands together. "Oh, this has to be something good. What have you got, you little hoodlum? **A PHONE? A LAPTOP? A TV?**"

I look down at the bag. "It would have to be a really small TV."

He seems stumped for a second, then shakes his massive head. "They make them small sometimes. Now, come on, open it. Before I get **ANGRY**."

So this isn't him angry now? He already looks like a giant muscly tomato.

His walkie-talkie crackles and a disembodied voice comes out. "Base to Julian."

The man rolls his eyes and answers. "Base, we've discussed this. My professional name is **J-DOG**."

"OK, Julian," the voice says. "We've got some aggro kicking off outside the birthday shop. Someone trying to return a card even though there's a greeting written inside it."

Julian spins round and looks back into the main part of the mall. OK, GOLDEN OPPORTUNITY. I quickly grab the head out of the bag and shove it behind the bin.

"J-DOG will be there in a minute," Julian grizzles. "Just got something to deal with here first."

He turns back to me and folds his arms again. "I'm going to ask you one more time.

OPEN. THE. BAG."

I sigh. "OK, fiiiiine."

Julian frowns into  the empty bag. "But there's nothing in there."

"That's what YOU think," I say. "But actually I use this bag to keep all my HOPES AND DREAMS for the future."

I pinched that bad boy off my mum. She has an empty money pot and says she uses it to store all the LOVE she has for her children. When Brandon moaned that it was really tiny, she sent him to take the bins out.

Julian narrows his eyes at me. "You're lucky there's a **CARD SITUATION** going on, otherwise I'd be taking you to the slammer."

I gasp. "The EnormoMall has a prison?"

"It's actually my office," he says. "But make no mistake," he points two fingers at his eyes, then one at me, "**I'LL BE WATCHING YOU.**"

Once angry J-Dog has power-walked around the corner, I stuff the head back into the bag and carry on. I hope he doesn't get Sam.

PREDATOR

I managed to film a quick FlipFlop in a far-flung corner of an American sweet-shop, acting all **ALIEN-Y** among the Jolly Ranchers, before I check my watch. There's only **TEN MINUTES** until I have to meet Sam. Time for one more.

Checking I'm not being spied on, I make my way up the escalator and look for my last location. **THE FOOD COURT?** No, too crowded. **THE TOY SHOP?** I'd probably get too distracted. Hang on a sec. What does that sign say?

OFFICES

There's a corridor heading off the main mall and I can't help but head down there. I feel like I've got a **SEVENTH SENSE** for things like this: seeing opportunities. My **SIXTH** sense is knowing when not to go in our bathroom at home.

Gripping my bag tight, I creep down the corridor. There are a few doors, some with signs and some without, but at the very end, on a door made from much fancier wood than the others, is a **BRASS PLAQUE** emblazoned with the name Sir Percival Hickenbottom.

YESSS!

I quickly put on the head and film myself walking up and down outside Sir Percival's office. This one is going to be **SO GOOD!** I'm about to stop, but decide I want to film a little more, so do another circuit.

SLAM!

I whack into the wall. OOF! I must have got confused. I take off the head and blink as my eyes get used to the bright light. Wait a second. Why is this wall black? And why does it smell like aftershave, coffee and ARMPIT SWEAT?

THE WAR OF THE WORLDS

"STOP!" Julian booms, but no way am I going to do that. I am GETTING OUT of this place. Once I'm outside the EnormoMall, there's nothing he can do.

The ESCALATORS are ahead. If I can get down them in good time, I'll have a chance.

"RON, GRAB HIM!" Julian shouts.

I see the man who must be Ron in front of the stairs. He's half the size of Julian and twice as old. He holds his arms out like a goalkeeper trying to save a penalty. My **SEVENTH SENSE** kicks in: the floors here are super shiny and slick. I look down and can see my reflection in them. **HERE GOES.**

I skid on my knees and the floor carries me squealing through the old man's legs.

"HAHAHA! EAT MY DUST, RON!"

But oh no, I can't stop and I'm heading right for the escalator **COMING UP** from the floor below! I flop on to the hard metal and am **IMMEDIATELY** carried back towards Julian and Ron.

Using the handrails, I pull myself up and **RUN** down the escalator the wrong way. A lady coming up squawks and calls me a "**HOOLIGAN**".

I quickly turn my head and see Ron has given up, but Julian is still pounding down the escalator towards me.

"Out of the way!" he yells. "I've got a **FUGITIVE** in my sights!"

I leap off the escalator, and before I can stop myself I **SMASH** into a stand giving out free samples of cocktail sausages.

"The suspect has upended the complimentary chipolatas; repeat, suspect

119

has upended the complimentary chipolatas,"
Julian pants into his walkie-talkie.

Something has happened. My feet are no
longer connected to the shiny floor. I look
down and I'm **SKIDDING** on the sausages.
And I can't stop! I skid faster and **FASTER**,
wobbling my arms around to stay upright.

I jump up straight away, but I'm **SOAKED.**
I look up at the giant naked statue holding a
trumpet and he seems to be laughing at me.

Julian splashes into the fountain after me,
so I clamber over the side and **RUN** as fast
as my sodden body will take me. The
entrance is ahead. **I'M GOING TO MAKE IT!
I'M GOING TO MAKE IT!**

A dark shape steps in front of me and
grabs me tight. No, I was **SO CLOSE!**

"You're not getting away this time, you
little alien," Sir Percival hisses.

THE SHOWDOWN

"When I said I had **PROOF** that this alien thing was a load of old bunk and hooey, I was talking about reports from **AIR TRAFFIC CONTROL** on the night of the supposed crash," I hear Hickenbottom moan from where he's addressing the crowd outside Grandma's shop. "But a stroke of luck landed me with something even more compelling this evening."

I'm sitting in the back of his fancy car with Julian. The doors are locked. **NO CHANCE OF ESCAPE.**

"All right, put your mask on, kid," Julian growls.

"**WHY?**" I moan.

"Because that's what the boss wants," he says. "Now, COME ON. Stick it over your head. Chop-chop."

I have no choice but to do as he asks. I hear the door open and I'm led out of the car.

"And now, ladies and gentlemen," Sir Percival drones. "Here are your SO-CALLED ALIENS."

I can hear people murmur as I'm pushed forwards.

"These children have perpetrated a great HOAX upon this town," he goes on. "And now it is time for them to face the music."

The papier mâché head is lifted off me.
It's getting dark now, but the crowd is lit
by nearby lamp-posts and among them
I see my family.

"OH, LENNY, I'm shocked," Mum gasps.

Brandon sniggers. "I'm not."

I see Grandma near the back, still with
her apron on. She looks really sad and it
makes my eyes go all prickly.

"WAIT!" I say,
shouting over the
noise. "I can
explain!"

"HE CAN EXPLAIN?!" Sir Percival guffaws. "Oh, I can't wait to hear this."

I turn and see Sam next to me in the dark, his mask still on. He must be so scared. Even more than me.

"We didn't mean to cause TROUBLE," I say. "It's just that my grandma's shop didn't have any people visiting. Sam's dad's bookshop too. And it was all because of Sir Shufflebottom's MegaMall."

"It's Hickenbottom," he snootily corrects me. "And EnormoMall."

"WHATEVER,"

I say. "Basically, we only did it because we wanted to save the town."

Sir Percival laughs again, clutching at his huge belly. "SAVE THE TOWN? That's so precious! I've heard it all now."

Sam's dad makes his way to the front, his **HAND UP** like he's asking permission to go for a wee.

"Actually, Sir Shufflebottom..."

"**SIR PERCIVAL HICKENBOTTOM!**"

"Sorry," says Sam's dad. "Actually, Sir Shufflebottom. I think you'll find most of us had big doubts about the alien thing."

I look around and see other people agreeing.

"David is right," says my mum. "Deep down, we knew there weren't **REALLY** any aliens. We just liked the magic of it. The idea that **ANYTHING IS POSSIBLE!**"

Loads of people agree now, some of them even clapping.

"And I just feel like you don't get that, Sir Slipperbottom," she goes on.

Sir Percival **GROANS** and rubs a hand down his face. I don't think this has gone how he thought.

"I **AGREE**." I hear a familiar voice near the back and have to squint to see Mr Greenford, along with Crumbs on a lead. "While I may not condone their actions, these boys have shown great imagination and, more importantly, **COMMUNITY SPIRIT**. I'm – uh." He stops and seems to think about what he's going to say next. "I'm proud to call them Fleurwood pupils."

This time a **BIG ROUND OF APPLAUSE** goes across the crowd. I even see Grandma doing one of those stick-your-fingers-in-your-mouth whistles.

"OK, son," says Sam's dad with a smile. "You can take the mask off now; you're not in trouble."

But Sam doesn't move. He just stands there in the shadows, **MOTIONLESS**.

"Sam?" says his dad, worry creeping into his voice.

I hear panting coming from the back of the crowd and see a YELLOW PUFF OF HAIR sprinting towards me.

Sam stands opposite, trying to catch his breath. "So ... sorry ... Lenny. Nearly ... caught ... escaped."

"Hang on a second," I say. "If you're there, then WHO IS THAT?"

I turn just in time to see the figure next to me raising its arms, then a **BRIGHT-GREEN LIGHT** beams from its eyes.

"Do not fear, earthlings," it says in a strange voice. **"I COME IN PEACE!"**

The crowd gasps and many start recording on their phones. A few run away, screaming.

"I come from the planet **JEZANDRIA** with a message of hope," it goes on.

"Never mind hope," Sir Percival yells. "We've got ourselves a **REAL ALIEN** here. I'm rich! Even more than I already was! **GRAB IT, BOYS!**"

Julian and Ron lurch out of the darkness and try to seize the alien.

"**NO!**"

I push the alien forwards, towards the crowd, who scatter out of the way. I don't know how this alien got here, or whether it knows what is going on. I just know I can't let Sir Percy get his mitts on the poor thing.

It doesn't seem to be able to run very fast. We're going to need something better. **AND THAT'S WHEN I SEE IT,** propped up against some railings near Dad.

"Come on, we're taking the **FLYING BIKE,**" I say. "You sit in the basket."

ESCAPE

We **TEAR** down the street on the bike and I press **TURBO 1** to get the speed up. Two cars begin to pull out and **CHASE** us. Time to crank it up to **TURBO 2**.

"HOLD ON TIGHT!"

I say to the alien as I hit TURBO 3. "I'm not going to let them take you, don't worry!"

But the cars are CLOSE now, and I can hear Sir Percival screaming something out of the window. I can't make out what it is. Something about "end". What's he talking about?

He says it again, and this time it's clearer.

"YOU'RE NOT GOING TO ESCAPE, YOU FOOLS! THAT WAY IS A DEAD END!"

Oh no! Of course! They still haven't fixed the bridge over Duggler's Ditch! I check around, but there is **NO OTHER WAY** to go.

"Oh, Dad," I moan. "Please let this be the one invention of yours that **ACTUALLY WORKS!**"

I turn it up to **TURBO 4** and try and remember what Dad said.

"I think it's the timing, Lenny. I feel like I need to hit Fly at the exact right moment when I get to **TURBO FIVE,** *but I keep missing it."*

Duggler's Ditch looms ahead. We're going to be there in no time. **TURBO 5.**

"STOP, YOU IDIOT! DON'T DAMAGE MY ALIEN!"

Sir Percival roars.

But I'm not going to stop. I can't.

The road below us disappears and I feel like I'm floating. The bike begins to come down as the sickening black hole of the ditch opens up. Here goes nothing. I smash the Fly button. The engine splutters and nothing happens. The bike drops lower.

"NO!"

I whack the button again.

BRRRRRROOO

SSSHH!

We zip upwards, **SOARING MAJESTICALLY** through the sky. The alien points at the huge full moon as we pass.

"OOOOOOOOH!"

We hit the road on the other side of the ditch and we skid this way, then that. I struggle to keep control of the bike, but we're heading for the woods and there's nothing I can do about it. The alien falls out of the basket and I'm thrown into a bush.

I stand up and survey the damage. I'm a bit scratched, but nothing too bad. Where is the alien though?

"Hello?" I call out. "Alien? Are you OK?"

I find the alien slumped against the tree. Its head has fallen off.

PHONE HOME

"Hang on a minute,"
I say. "Jess?"

She sits up and groans,
waving sheepishly.
"All right, fine,
you got me."

CRUNCH, CRUNCH, CRUNCH.

"I know you're in there!" Sir Percival shouts. "Come out now and make it easier on yourselves!"

We give each other a look. Neither of us are ever going to come out now. We creep deeper into the woods. It's **DARK AND SCARY,** but not as scary as Sir Percy and his huge goons.

We find a thick bush and crouch behind it while he stomps further away from us.

"**THAT WAS REALLY COOL,**" I whisper.

Jess nods as if to say "obviously".

"I asked your dad if I could borrow his

VOICE TRANSFORMER," she explains. "Then it was just a case of adding those cool lights to the mask."

I sigh. "Sorry for lying to you. We were going to tell you, we just never found the right time."

"Well, you **SHOULD** be sorry," she says. "I knew it was you, right from when I first heard about it. After we met at your grandma's place, I followed you and **EAVESDROPPED** on your plans. I wanted to catch you in the act and shame you, but then that guy grabbed me and that was that. Then, when I heard your reasons for doing it,

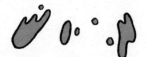

I couldn't stay mad at you. You really **DID** save the town."

We both smile. "Shall we hug it out?" I ask. "**ABSOLUTELY NOT**," says Jess.

We pick our way through the woods and find ourselves back on the main street. When Sam sees us, he runs over and hugs me, then gives Jess a firm handshake.

"I had a feeling it was you," he says.

She socks him on the arm. "You trying to say I remind you of an **EXTRATERRESTRIAL**, Sam?"

Sir Percival stumbles out of the woods with twigs sticking out of his hair. "**AHA!**

I caught you! Hang on a minute, what happened to the alien?"

"In the woods at the crash site," I say. "I think it's going to use **SPACE MAGIC** to put its ship back together and fly home, so you'd better be quick."

Sir Percival nods, then sprints back into the woods.

EEEEEEEEAAAAAOOWWWW.

We all giggle as Sir Percy's terrified screams ring out through the night air.

A FEW DAYS LATER

Normally, the last day of the summer holidays is the most **DEPRESSING** day of the year, but this one isn't.

Me, Sam and Jess are walking through town. Each of us has a Patented Trademark Lenny Lemmon Quadruple Super Scooper

from Grandma's place and there are people EVERYWHERE.

"It's funny, isn't it?" I say. "All it took to remind people how COOL our town is was some pretend aliens."

"I'm happy it has all worked out," says Sam. "The shop is doing very well. But please, don't EVER come up with any more ideas like that."

Jess chuckles. "I think you know that's not going to happen, Sam."

I stop and look up at the sky. Even though it's daylight, I can still see the faint wisp of the MOON, that same moon Jess and I

seemed to get close enough to touch the other night.

"Makes you wonder though, doesn't it?" I say. "WHAT ELSE MIGHT BE UP THERE?"

"Your dad's an inventor," says Jess. "Why don't you get him to build us a SPACE ROCKET?"

"No," says Sam.

"OH, YEAH!" I say. "We could visit the moon and bring back some cheese!"

"No," says Sam.

"Moon schmoon, I want to go to Jupiter!" says Jess.

"NO!" says Sam.

"One small step for Sam," I say.

"One giant leap for Samkind," Jess fills in.

And we **LAUGH**. Even Sam does, a bit.

Ahh. I love my friends. I love my life. **I LOVE MY TOWN**.

Have you read?

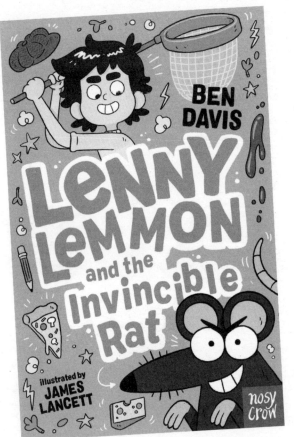

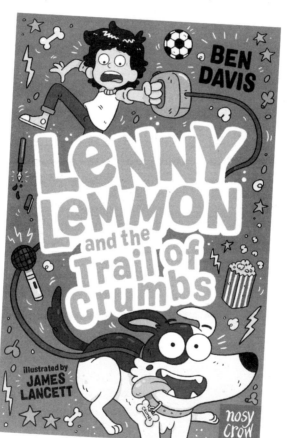